Herbert Loves Sherbet

by **Joanie Leopold**

illustrated by **Jim Steck**

For James and Adela,
who have reawakened so many of my dreams

Published by Slow Tag Press
2124 Center Avenue, Northbrook, Illinois 60062
stories@slowtagpress.com
www.slowtagpress.com

•

Library of Congress Control Number 2016915978
ISBN: 0-9981425-0-6
ISBN 13: 978-0-9981425-0-0

•

Printed in PRC

Little Herbert Clark loved sherbet.
He dreamed of how it tasted.
If he went three meals without some,
He felt the day was wasted.

When he woke up every morning
He gave Mom a kiss and squeeze.
When she asked his choice for breakfast
He said, "Sherbet, if you please."

3

"Some sherbet with my ham and eggs,
One scoop beside my waffle.
I'll even have some in a mug.
Without it, I'd feel awful."

"Now, Herb," his mother scolded him.
"You need healthy things to eat."
So she poured a glass of cocoa
And served steaming Cream of Wheat.

Mom filled the house with yummy foods.
Herb always cleaned his dishes.
But every chance he got he'd talk
About his sherbet wishes.

Whenever it was hot or cold
Or sunny, bright or cloudy,
At holidays and party time
Herb asked for sherbet loudly.

He asked for sherbet in his lunch,
For a bedtime snack at night.
But, dinner was the only time
He got his sherbet bite.

6

One day while Mom was dishing out
His scoop of lemon sherbet
She said, "Dad and I just won a trip.
We leave tomorrow, Herbert."

"Grandma Bess is coming here,
And she will be delighted
To play your games and serve you treats."
Wow! Herbert was excited.

As he danced around the kitchen
His eyes began to flicker.
"Gran always gives me what I want.
I think that I can trick her."

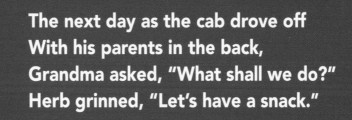

The next day as the cab drove off
With his parents in the back,
Grandma asked, "What shall we do?"
Herb grinned, "Let's have a snack."

So Grandma served a plate of fruit
While Herbert just looked doleful.
"Don't fret," she soothed. "What would you like?"
"Some sherbet please – a bowlful."

At twelve o'clock he had his lunch,
And you just couldn't beat it.
The sherbet scoops were piled so high
He had to stand to eat it.

His friends all came to visit him
Where Gran served bowls so loaded
That when they'd eaten all they could
They felt like they'd exploded.

11

By evening Herbert was content.
His plan looked like a winner
Until he heard his grandma say,
"I'll grill some trout for dinner."

"Hey, Grandma," Herbert called in fear,
"Fish always makes me queasy.
Instead of trout I guess you know
It's sherbet that would please me."

"Sounds good to me," Grandma agreed.
"I bet it tastes delicious."
She smiled at him and winked one eye.
Could Grandma be suspicious?

The next day Herbert ate his fill.
Each bite was one to savor.
He couldn't stop until he had
Tried every sherbet flavor.

By morning three when he awoke
Herb smiled when he sniffed bacon.
Some real food would taste fine now.
Smelled good what she was makin'.

While Gran had bacon with her eggs
Herb dropped down at the table.
He tried to clean his sherbet bowl,
But he just wasn't able.

"You're smart!" She smiled, "Don't get too full.
Save room inside that tummy.
Your sherbet lunch is raspberry.
Now doesn't that sound yummy?"

At lunch Herb sat with feet propped up
While kids around were munching.
"I'm so relaxed at school today
That I think I'll skip lunching."

All night long while Herbert slept
He dreamed he smelled a stew on.
"Enough!" he cried when he awoke.
"I need food I can chew on."

18

Peach sherbet was his breakfast fare.
Then more at noon and six.
But what Herb really wanted most
Were crunchy carrot sticks.

With each big bowl his grandma said,
"A brand new flavor. Try it."
How could he tell his dear sweet gran
To stop this sherbet diet?

19

He fed the sherbet to his dog.
He poured it down the gutter.
The flower garden got a bowl.
His belly was aflutter.

At last his mom and dad came home.
They got a joyous greeting.
"Let's celebrate," said Herbert Clark,
"With songs and lots of eating."

"Yes, let's!" They hugged and spun him 'round.
"We all can have some sherbet."
"If you don't mind, I'd much prefer
Some broccoli," said Herbert.

His parents did a double take.
Could this boy be their child?
But Gran, who didn't say a word,
Just winked one eye and smiled.

Special thanks to

Susie Haubenstock & Brian Mazzaferri

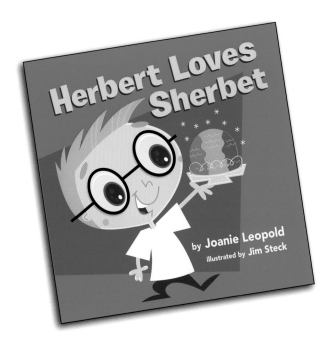

Order your copy today at

www.Amazon.com

www.SlowTagPress.com